WALLY
the Wobbling Wellington

Wally was a wellington. A bright-yellow wellington. And he had a brother called Willy.

Willy was always clean – and very sensible.

But Wally wasn't.
He was always muddy and wet.
He was the welly that was lost
or untidy...

He was the welly...
that **wobbled.**

Wobble! Wobble!

Now, the reason Wally wobbled
was because he was ticklish.

TERRIBLY TICKLISH!

The doormat tickled him...

WE

The fluffy carpet in the hall tickled him...

Even Felix the Fly tickled him,
although Felix happily tickled **anyone**!

But that was nothing compared to

THE SOCKS!

$\mathbf{T}$hen, just at that moment,
THE SOCKS came along.

They were looking for someone to tickle.

"**OH, NO!**" gasped Wally.

"Hello, Wally!" giggled Sophie Sock.
"**Got** you!" joined in Sarah Sock.

And together they tickled and tickled!

"YEE HA... OHH...
HA HA, HOO HA!"

Wally giggled and wriggled,
and squiggled, and...
WHOOPS!

Wally wobbled out of the door and into the garden.

I must find a cure for my ticklishness, he thought
as he wobbled off down the garden path.

WIBBLY WOBBLY...
SQUIGGLY SQUELCH...
SLIP SLIDE AND...

straight into a puddle!

SPLOSH!!

"**W**atch out!" Spicer the Spider piped up.

"Sorry!" said Wally. "But I'm looking for
a cure for my ticklishness."

"I could **tire** out your tickle!"
offered Spicer, dropping to the ground.

And with his eight hairy legs,
Spicer tickled as hard as he could.

HA HA HA!

"Am I cured?" asked Wally,
with no sign of a wobble.

Then a feather drifted on to his nose.

"Ooh, it tickles!" laughed Wally...
and wobbled.

HEE HEE HEE!

What are **you** wobbling about?" asked Snodgrass the Snail, with one or two www.wobbles of his own!

"I'm tired of being ticklish!" said Wally, sighing.

"But you wouldn't **BE** tickly if you were...

SLIPPERY!" said Snodgrass.

And he covered poor Wally...

in SLIME!

Sophie and Sarah started running towards him.
"Give them the slip!" said Snodgrass, and winked.

But Wally could do nothing **else**!

He **SLIPPED**... and he **SLID**!

"Whoops! Look out!"

WIBBLY WOBBLY
SQUIGGLY SQUELCH!

SCHLOOP!

He slid straight into Bertha the Barrel.

"Not so fast!" said Bertha, who was up to her elbows in water.

"The **SOCKS** are after me!" wailed Wally. He explained about being tickly, slippery and...

still very WOBBLY!

BONK!!

"**W**e need to find a cure for your ticklishness," said Bertha, as she pulled out a large, wet book.

"Let me see now," she said.

"**R... for Rudeness...**
S... for Silliness...
Here we are!
T... for Ticklishness!"

Bertha's book had a cure for everything, and the answer was always the same.

Washing.
   Washing.
         And **more** washing!

Poor Wally! He got soap in his eyes and soap in his ears, while Bertha sang at the top of her voice: "Rub-a-dub-dub! Scrub Wally in the tub!"

Bertha sponged him and rubbed him, soaped and scrubbed him... Then **SQUEEZED** him until he was dry.

SCRUB! SCRUB!

"Gosh!" he said, when at **last** it was over.

"I'm all clean and shiny...

just like my brother Willy!"

B**ut then THE SOCKS** came along!

And Bertha decided to teach those two naughty girls a lesson...

"I don't like it when it's two against one," she said firmly.

So she grabbed Sophie with one hand and Sarah with the other...

AND SHE PLUNGED THEM BOTH INTO THE WATER!

"Rub-a-dub-dub, two **SOCKS** in the tub!" she sang.

SCRUB!

SCRUB!

SCRUB!

Then Bertha
SQUEEZED
Sarah out and **HID** her inside Wally!

"Where's Sarah?" asked Sophie,
as Bertha fished her out of the water.

She didn't know that Bertha
had **hidden** Sarah...

"**W**here's **who**?" asked Bertha cheekily, trying to look surprised.

"Sarah? Oh, didn't you know? One sock **ALWAYS** gets lost in the wash!"

"These things... just happen," added Snodgrass wisely, as he wobbled by...

But, not liking at all what had just "happened",
Sophie started to cry.

"**D**on't cry, Sophie," said Wally,
"Sarah's in **here**!"

"Thank you, Willy!"
the Socks said together.

"I'm not Willy!" laughed Wally, "I'm Wally!"
"He just **LOOKS** like me... for once" said
Willy in delight, as he marched over to share
in all the fun.

"But Wally – you're no longer wobbly!" said Sarah.
"Or ticklish!" added Sophie.

And, however hard they tried to wiggle and giggle,
Bertha had cured his tickle...

... leaving only the tiniest wobble.

Come and play hide and seek with us at...

www.hoohahouse.com

It's free to become a Hoo Ha House Mate...

Join our gang and you will receive:

Hoo Ha
Wobbly Eye Badge

Colouring Cards

Christmas Cards

Hoo Ha House Mate
Membership Certificate

Hoo Ha Letters

50% off voucher

To be completed by parent/guardian

(Please be assured we will never give your personal information to 3rd parties)

I would like (child's name) [ ] to become a House Mate.

Child's date of birth [DD] [MM] [YYYY]

Please send their free goodies care of parent/guardian to

Your Name [ ]

Address [ ]

[ ]

Town/City [ ]   Post Code [ ] [ ]

I would like to be kept up-to-date with exciting news and offers via text or email.

Mobile [ ]

Email [ ]

Open to the residents of the UK and Northern Ireland only.

Allow 28 days for delivery. We reserve the right to withdraw or change the terms of this offer at any time.

For full terms & conditions, privacy policy and to check that the offer details are still correct please visit

www.hoohahouse.com/housemateoffer.

Return this whole page to:

I'm a Hoo Ha House Mate, c/o Mystical Productions, 1 Great Cumberland Place, London, W1H 7AL